DARK CLAW

Road Rage

May the Guiding Paw be with you!

Shoo Rayner

Hodder
Children's
Books

First published in Great Britain in 2002
by Hodder Children's Books

10 9 8 7 6 5 4

The right of
Shoo Rayner to be identified as the Author of
the Work has been asserted by him in accordance with the Copyright,
Designs and Patents Act 1988.

A Catalogue record for this book is available from the
British Library

ISBN 0 340 81755 0

Printed and bound in Great Britain by
Bookmarque Limited, Croydon, Surrey

The paper and board used in this paperback by Hodder Children's
Books are natural recyclable products made from wood grown in
sustainable forests. The manufacturing processes conform to the
environmental regulations of the country of origin.

Hodder Children's Books
a division of Hodder Headline Limited
338 Euston Road
London NW1 3BH

Chapter 1

Rocket engines screamed.
The spacecraft rattled and shook.
For three minutes it was hard to
move or breathe.

But as they headed deep into space,
the passengers relaxed.

Onlee One, Chin Chee and Hammee were on their way to the Tunnel-Mazing championships in Muss Vegas on the planet Dice.

The three friends made a brilliant team. They'd been allowed to compete, even though they were still at school.

Hammee spoke with a mouth full of peanuts. "I still can't believe we're really going to the Championships."

Chin Chee laughed. "We wouldn't be going at all, if Onlee One hadn't eaten Dark Claw's piece of Fworgonzola cheese."

Onlee One smiled and thought to himself:

If I *hadn't* eaten it, *none* of us would be here at all!

Onlee One had eaten the rare, and very smelly Fworgonzola, and had gained an incredible sense of smell. This had ruined the evil Dark Claw's deadly plan to destroy the whole of the Muss race.*

Onlee One shuddered. Dark Claw had come so close to destroying them all.

"I wonder what he's planning now," he thought as he watched Planet Muss fade into the distance.

*See book 1 Tunnel Mazers.

Chapter 2

Somewhere else in space, a Pi-rat ship cruised towards the landing bay of Dark Claw's secret base, Dark Moon.

Dark Claw smiled to himself.
"At last, they have come."

He swept along the corridors to meet
the Pi-rat crew in the landing bay.

Their leader was a tall, striking Ratess.
She swaggered up to Dark Claw and
introduced herself.

I am Ratuschka.
We hear you need
some help.

Dark Claw studied her closely.
"There's a Muss I need to be rid of,"
he growled.

Ratuschka's eyes glowed with
pleasure.

Getting rid of
Muss is what we
do best!

Later, in the control room,
they watched secretly filmed video of
Onlee One and his friends.
Dark Claw pointed at Onlee One.

"He is the special one!" he hissed.
"But you can deal with the other
two as well."

Dark Claw went through the plan to capture him.

"Make sure you bring him back alive.
I want to watch his final moments!"

Ratuschka smirked. She and her crew
were going to enjoy this job.

Leave it to us!

Chapter 3

Muss Vegas isn't called "Vacation City" for nothing. It's shiny and glitzy, and all the banners were out for the Inter Stellar Tunnel-Mazing Championships.

The opening ceremony was amazing. Chancellor Brandling had come to watch and give the prizes. She spotted Onlee One in the crowd and went to speak with him.

"We meet again!" she said. "Good luck, you are playing against the the very best now!"

Onlee One's reply was drowned by an incredible noise. The stadium filled with dust.

With throbbing engines, five huge Road Ragers rolled into the stadium. They were giant wheels. From each of them, loud music blared.

The sound died away and the drivers climbed out. They were Pi-rats!

Ratuschka waited for the crowd to hush before she spoke.

We wanna play too!

Rats usually mean trouble, and no one wanted to upset them. But all drivers should have been entered for the competition months before.

Brandling took charge and welcomed the newcomers.

In the spirit of friendship between Muss and Rats, we welcome you and look forward to your good and fair competition.

Ratuschka met Onlee One's eyes.
She smiled.

Onlee One shivered and turned
to his friends.

"I don't trust this lot," he said.

Chapter 4

Tunnel-mazing is simple.
You go in one hole…

…go round a maze …

…and come out of
another hole.

Cheeses are placed at different exit
holes. In total darkness, you have to
sniff your way to the right exit!

Thanks to the Fworgonzola, Onlee One now had the best sense of smell of any Muss alive. He also had the ability to draw a map of the maze in his head, as he went along.

"Something's not right," he whispered to his friends. There's a new smell. Someone's dug a new hole since we last came along here."

A little further on, a shaft of light fell from the roof of the tunnel.

"We came down this tunnel five minutes ago," said Onlee One. "This hole wasn't here then."

"Are you sure?" whispered Chin Chee.

Hammee tutted.

"Wait here," said Onlee One. "I'll see what happens a bit further on."

He edged forwards into the darkness.
Then his whiskers bristled. Something
was very wrong.

He was moving through the tunnel
when he heard a scuffling noise behind
him. He turned and ran back the way
he had come. His friends had gone.
Only the smell of Rats hung in the air.

Onlee One heard a faint cry.
It was Hammee calling for help.

Onlee One peered out of the hole.
The competition had begun. His team
would be disqualified, but that didn't
matter now.

Twenty metres away, Hammee and
Chin Chee were being bundled into
two Road Ragers.

Onlee One scrambled up the side of the
hole, but he was too late.
The Road Ragers were already
storming off in a cloud of dust.

He would never catch them up.

Chapter 5

In the middle of the settling dust, an engine choked. One of the Rats had flooded his motor. He'd have to wait a minute before he could get it started.

The Road Rager was parked next to a flag pole. Onlee One crept up behind it without being seen.

He let down the flag and used the rope
to tie the Road Rager to the pole.

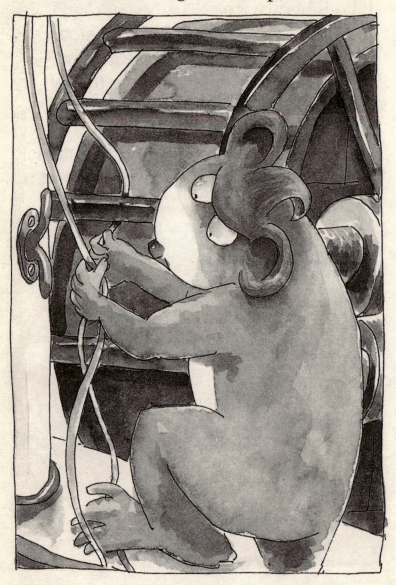

The Rat tried the
engine again.
It coughed twice,
and roared into life.

But the wheel was tied and couldn't
turn. The insides, including the driver,
turned instead. The Rat spun round
fifty times before the engine cut out!

He fell out of his seat and lay on the ground, holding his stomach and groaning. He wasn't going anywhere in a hurry!

Quickly, Onlee One untied the rope and climbed into the Road Rager. He talked himself through the controls.

I guess I turn this... and squeeze this... and put my foot down on this...and...woooooah!

Urgh!

Chapter 6

Onlee One soon caught up the other Road Ragers, which were headed straight for a lake.

"They'll have to stop there," he thought.

But he was wrong. As they hit the water, balloons blew up on the wheels, and they drove right across the water!

At the water's edge, Onlee One stopped and looked at the control panel. He pressed a likely looking button.

Instead of balloons, he was deafened by the loudest music he'd ever heard! The whole machine shook in time with the beat.

Another button had
a picture like a wave.
Onlee One pressed it…

With a loud woosh, the balloons began
to fill with air. He felt himself lifted on
to the surface of the water.

Pishhh!

As Onlee One skittered across the surface of the lake, he could see the others in the distance.

They had slowed right down, and were circling as if they didn't know which way to go.

Then they made their minds up and zoomed off into the desert.

When Onlee One reached the same place, he stopped, switched off the engine and climbed out.

"Now, why did they stop here?"
he thought. He sniffed the breeze.
There were two different rat smells in
the air. He laughed out loud.
"They've gone the wrong way!"

One rat smell came from the direction the gang had just gone in.

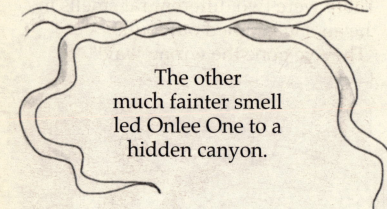

The other
much fainter smell
led Onlee One to a
hidden canyon.

At the mouth of the canyon, a guard lay asleep in the sun. And there, in the shadows, was the Pi-rats' spaceship.

Onlee One revved the engine and drove at the spaceship's boarding ramp.

Once inside, he jabbed the ramp shutter button. As the ramp lifted up, he saw the guard running towards the ship, calling out, "Hey, wait for me!"

Too late, chum!

Chapter 7

The inside of the spaceship was a mess. There was rubbish everywhere. It hadn't been tidied up for years. Onlee One held his nose. "Phew, it stinks!"

He sat in the cockpit and worked out the flight system. Luckily, spaceship controls are pretty much the same wherever you go.

The guard was still banging on the side of the ship as Onlee One started up the engines.

Carefully, he nosed out of the canyon. He flew a couple of metres off the ground, and headed out after the Road Ragers.

Chapter 8

Ratuschka's crew were completely lost. They argued over whose fault it was.

"Where's Rabies?" asked Ratuschka. "He knew the way."

"He was right behind us at the Lake," said Anouschka. "Maybe he's gone to get the ship. Maybe he'll come looking for us."

Nearby, Hammee and Chin Chee were tied to a large rock. Chin Chee listened to the Rats, hoping to find out why they had been taken prisoner.

"I'm hungry!" Hammee whined.

Chin Chee dug her elbow in his ribs. "You're always hungry... Sshh!"

Suddenly, the rats were cheering.
Chin Chee looked up to see why.
The Pi-rat ship was floating across
the desert towards them.

Her heart sank.
Where would the
gang take
them to now?

The Pi-rats waved and cheered as the first laser blast parted Ratuschka's hair!

Pow!

They all ducked and the rest of the blasts shot over their heads.

Ziing!

Peeeow!

Zap!

"Hey! Why's Karlov shooting at us?" yelled Ratuschka.
"Wait till I get hold of him!"

An echoey voice boomed out of the
ship's speaker system.

> If you want this ship
> back, untie those two and return
> to Muss Vegas now.

Hammee and Chin Chee cheered.

> It's Onlee One!

The Pi-rats started arguing again.

"This is all your fault!"
Ratushka screamed.

"I didn't do nuffin!"
Ratoo yelled back.

The voice from the ship called again.

You have ten
seconds until I start
firing again!

Ratuschka stood up with her paws in the air. "OK! OK!" She shouted.

Climbing into her Road Rager, she spat orders at her crew.

Untie those two and let's get out of here!

Chapter 9

"Phew! That was close." said Chin Chee.

The three friends were together again in the Pi-rat ship. Chin Chee told Onlee One what she had heard.

The Pi-rats are working for Dark Claw. They took us as hostages to make you go back to Dark Moon to save us. I hate to think what Dark Claw wants to do to you.

"I know what I'd like to do to him!" said Hammee. He was searching the spaceship's lockers for food.

He opened a tin and sniffed it.

Ugh! I'm not eating any of this stuff! It's disgusting.

The other two smiled. The food had to be bad. Hammee would eat almost anything "Let's get back to civilisation!" laughed Onlee One.

As they flew back to Muss Vegas, they saw the Road Ragers down below them.

"We'll get there before them," said Onlee One. "We can tell Brandling what happened. She'll know what to do for the best."

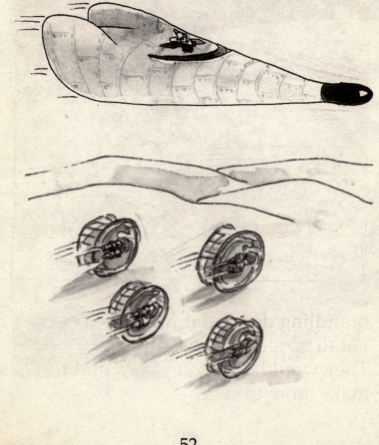

Chapter 9

In the stadium, a huge crowd watched as the Pi-rats returned.

Brandling decided it would be best not to upset the Rats any more. They would only come back and make more trouble.

She spoke to Ratuschka in private.

No real harm has been done here. You are free to go, but you will leave your Road Ragers behind. We shall have some sport with them.

Ratuschka's eyes narrowed. There had to be a catch.

How do I know you won't shoot us down as soon as we are away from here?

Brandling gave her a thin, golden disc.
It was a transmitter passport.
"This will see you safely home.
No one will bother you while it is
switched on."

Ratuschka examined the disc and
smiled. Brandling spoke again.

Give your master
this message: If he wishes
harm to any Muss, he will
answer to me!

Ratuschka and her gang climbed
aboard their ship and flew away. When
it was just a tiny dot in the sky
Brandling turned to the crowd.

The crowd roared with delight. They were going to get some sporting action after all!

Of course, Onlee One had a head start on the other drivers... no one else had ever driven a Road Rager before! No one was surprised when Onlee crossed the finish line first.

Brandling placed the medal round his neck and smiled.

"It's so nice to be a winner, isn't it?" she said. "Now, smile for the cameras!"

Chapter 10

Meanwhile, on Dark Moon, the Pi-rats stood before Dark Claw. They hung their heads in shame.

"You fools. You have failed me. Now I will have to think of another way to get my revenge."

"Sorry, Dark Claw," whined Ratuschka. "We did our best."

She took the golden disc from her
pocket and showed it to Dark Claw.

Have you seen the Dark Claw Website?

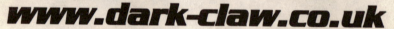

www.dark-claw.co.uk

Shoo Rayner designed and built the Dark Claw Website himself, while he was writing the Dark Claw stories. It is packed full of games and background stories about the worlds of Onlee One, his friends and his enemies!

Why is Dark Claw so angry?
Why does he want to destroy the Muss?

 Where in the Universe is the planet Muss?
What is Litterbox? What is Kimono?

What is it like at the Tan Monastery School?
Why do the beds squeak?

All this and more. If you're a Dark Claw fan, you'll love the Dark Claw website. It's all part of the story!

★ ★ ★ ★ ★

If you enjoyed this book you'll want to read the other books in the Dark Claw Saga.

Tunnel Mazers
0 340 81754 2
The one with the very
smelly cheese!

Road Rage
0 340 81755 0
The one with the cool
racing machines!

Rat Trap
0 340 81756 9
The one with invisible
space ships!

Breakout!
0 340 81757 7
The one with nowhere
left to go!

The Guiding Paw
0 340 81758 5
The one with the Muss-
eating jellyfish!

The Black Hole
0 340 81759 3
The one with the end
of the story!

Find out more about Shoo Rayner and his other fantastic books at www.shoo-rayner.co.uk

If you enjoyed this book you'll love these other books by Shoo Rayner and Hodder Children's Books

The Rex Files

(Seriously weird!)

0 340 71432 8   The Life-Snatcher
0 340 71466 2   The Phantom Bantam
0 340 71467 0   The Bermuda Triangle
0 340 71468 9   The Shredder
0 340 71469 7   The Frightened Forest
0 340 71470 0   The Baa-Baa Club

Or what about the wonderful
Ginger Ninja?

0 340 61955 4   The Ginger Ninja
0 340 61956 2   The Return of Tiddles
0 340 61957 0   The Dance of the Apple Dumplings
0 340 61958 9   St Felix for the Cup
0 340 69379 7   World Cup Winners
0 340 69380 0   Three's a Crowd

And don't forget SUPERDAD!
(He's a bit soft really!)

0 7500 2694 4   Superdad
0 7500 2706 1   Superdad the SuperHero

Phone 012345 400414 and have a credit card ready
Email orders to: orders@bookpoint.co.uk
Please allow the following for postage and packing:
UK & BFPO – £1.00 for the first book, 50p for the second book, and 30p for
each additional book ordered up to a maximum charge of £3.00.
OVERSEAS & EIRE – £2.00 for the first book, £1.00 for the second book,
and 50p for each additional book.